PUFFIN BOOKS
Published by the Penguin Group: London, New York, Australia, Canada, India, Ireland, New Zealand and South Africa
Penguin Books Ltd, Registered Offices: 80 Strand, London WC2R 0RL, England

puffinbooks.com

First published by Gullane Children's Books 2002
Published in Puffin Books 2004, 2006
This edition produced for The Book People Ltd, Hall Wood Avenue, Haydock, St Helens, WA11 9UL, 2009
1 3 5 7 9 10 8 6 4 2
Text copyright © Ian Whybrow, 2002, 2006, 2009
Illustrations copyright © Adrian Reynolds, 2002, 2006, 2009
Made and printed in China
ISBN: 978-0-141-33035-8

Romp
in the
Swamp

Ian Whybrow and **Adrian Reynolds**

PUFFIN

Mum and Nan were taking Sam to see her new school. That was why Harry and the dinosaurs had to go and play with some girl called Charlie.

Harry called their names but
the dinosaurs were hiding.

"Don't let Charlie play with us, Harry," said Apatosaurus.
"She might do bending on our legs," said Anchisaurus.
"She might chew our tails," said Triceratops.
"She won't understand about dinosaurs," said Scelidosaurus.

"Don't worry," said Harry. "You get in the bucket.
I won't let anyone else play with *my* dinosaurs."

"What took you so long, slowcoach?" said Sam.
"None of your business!" said Harry.
Good thing Nan sat between them.

Charlie and her mum came to the door to meet Harry.
Harry hid the dinosaurs behind his back.

"Goodbye!" called Mum. "Have a good time!"
Harry and the dinosaurs didn't think they would.

Charlie went inside and
sat on the sofa with her toys.

Harry sat at the other end of the sofa.
He guarded the dinosaurs and wouldn't speak.

Then Charlie went off
and found a big basket.
In went her dumper truck
and her tractor.

In went some cushions,
in went some boxes.

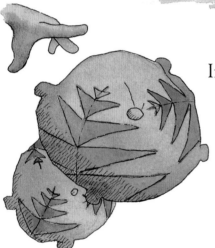

In went some pans
and some plants and
some string.

Harry and the dinosaurs
followed her into the garden.
  "What is she doing?"
whispered Harry.

"She's making a primeval forest!" said Anchisaurus.
"And a primordial swamp!" said Triceratops.
"That looks fun!" said Stegosaurus.

"Hisssssss"

went the hose like a great big snake.

"Look out!" Harry shouted.
"That snake might bite us!
Oh no, he's squeezing
Tyrannosaurus!
Quick! Save him!"

Harry and the dinosaurs joined in the noisy game.
Anchisaurus went crash with the tractor.
Scelidosaurus went bump with the dumper truck.
Apatosaurus and Triceratops made a strong
snake-lead out of string.
Stegosaurus grabbed the snake's tail.

"Help me with the snake cage!" shouted Charlie.
Whump went the snake cage and
captured the snake!

Then everyone did a noisy capture-dance.

"Hooray!" said Charlie. "What shall we do now?"
"Let's all have a feast!" said Harry.

"Would you like to play with
Charlie another day?" called Mum.
"Definitely!" said Harry.
"Definitely!" said the dinosaurs.

ENDOSAURUS